Under The Amish Trees

Terri Downes

Published by Trellis Publishing, 2021.

UNDER THE AMISH TREES

First edition. July 13, 2021.

Copyright © 2021 Terri Downes.

ISBN: 979-8224535668

Written by Terri Downes.

UNDER THE AMISH TREES

TERRI DOWNES

It had been a while since the last barn raising, and Matthew had almost forgotten how much he enjoyed them. The social element was fun, but it was working together, building something, that felt so good, that uplifted his soul and left it singing.

It had been hot today, and he felt sticky with sweat and tired all the way through, in a way that hinted at some stiffness tomorrow. Not much, as Matthew had plenty of heavy lifting to do every day at the farm, and he would be in a poor state if a barn raising set him back too much.

Still, he would sleep very well tonight... and he needed something cold.

The table that had been used to serve lunch had been cleared earlier, but there were jugs of water and iced tea set up at one end, being poured out by the expansively beaming Mrs. Annie Simon, who seemed thrilled at her family's new barn. As Matthew approached the table, however, he heard a baby start crying somewhere in the house. Annie stepped away from the table with a worried expression and beckoned to another of the women to take over from her.

Matthew's insides gave a jump as he saw who now stood at the table; his mouth, already dry, felt as though it were full of sand.

"Water – " his voice came out as a croak and he coughed hastily. "Um, water, please – " no better.

Lovina smiled politely at him.

"You sound like you've been wandering in the desert," she commented, placing an invitingly condensed glass of water before him.

Matthew drank half of it before he answered.

"Not quite that dire," he said.

He did not tell her that he had, in fact, once spent time in a desert, and had felt the dry, searing heat envelop him as though he had just opened the world's largest oven door, and that he had slept under the stars, which had been far more beautiful than he had been able to appreciate at the time.

Such things were not to be spoken of between them.

"Tiring work," Lovina added, nodding towards the almost-finished barn.

Matthew nodded. And then, unbidden, her words recalled a memory long buried. He grinned.

"Yes," he said recklessly, "but it's the *most best* kind of tired."

Lovina paused for a moment – then laughed, her face lighting with recognition. But then she looked over Matthew's shoulder, and her face fell. She frowned. Turning, Matthew followed her gaze, and saw his cousin.

Thomas was leaning back against a gatepost across the yard. His posture was languid and rakish, his smile almost a smirk, as he talked to the girl standing beside him. The girl who Matthew recognized now as Lovina's sister Tessa.

He watched the pair for a moment, wondering... he could not see anything obviously untoward. He turned back to Lovina, but she had already started busying herself with putting the dirty glasses in a tub to be washed, and he knew that the small moment they had shared, an echo of so many others, was over.

***

Whoompf.

Bright, copper-colored shapes flew up above Matthew's head as he landed backwards in the pile of leaves, his short legs kicking up over his head in delight.

He turned and saw that Lovina had vanished, but a rustling in another pile gave away her position. A small giggle floated up.

"Lovina?" he called, pretending he did not know where she was.

Another giggle. Matthew decided that he could not be too hard on her. She was only five; he, on the other hand, was six, old enough to know that you are not supposed to giggle when you hide from people.

He walked forward quietly, placing each foot down heel-first to muffle his steps. As he reached the giggling pile, he reached down, scooped up a handful of leaves, and then jumped in front of the pile, showering them over Lovina.

"Got you!" he yelled.

She pouted, and tried to fight off the leaves as they landed on her. Matthew thought she should leave them. The orange looked nice with her pink cheeks, yellow hair and blue dress. She looked like a rainbow. He offered her a hand to help her out of the pile.

"How do you find me so fast?" she demanded.

"You have to stop laughing," explained Matthew as they walked on, Lovina occasionally darting forward to catch a leaf before it reached the ground.

It was fall, and the small beech wood that stretched along the land between their parents' farms had slowly been turning yellow and orange, brighter and brighter – until the leaves, grown heavy with color, began to fall to the ground below. Matthew and Lovina had both begged to be allowed to go play today, as the forest was exactly at that perfect moment when there was brightness both above and below, as though the forest were a golden hall in Heaven, and the leaves were still piled in big, crunchy drifts, before the rain came and washed them into mush.

Matthew had had a harder time getting permission than Lovina. She said his parents were "strict" - he was not sure what that meant, but he knew that he was not allowed to do as many things as the other children his age. Even when he had finished all his chores, he was not always allowed out, but had to sit quietly at home. Today, though, he had caught his mother in a good mood, and she had agreed.

"Are you tired?" he asked Lovina, aware that they had been playing for a while now.

"A bit," she said, pausing to step again on an especially crunchy leaf. "But it's the *most best* kind of tired."

He stopped himself from correcting her grammar, reminding himself again of her youth and ignorance.

"It is," he agreed. And Lovina, he thought, might be the most best person he knew.

***

Dusk was beginning to fall, the sky deepening into a creamy purple, by the time Matthew and Thomas reached the lane that led to home. Matthew drew in a deep breath, feeling as though he could bask in the gentle coolness and falling quiet until they reached the farmhouse.

But Thomas was antsy, as usual, and kept humming and kicking at the path as they walked, raising clouds of dust. Matthew sighed inwardly. His cousin had been staying with him for several months now, and he had yet to acquire the sense of responsibility his father had hoped the change would bring to him. Uncle Jesse had grown up a farmer, and worried that his seventeen year old son's frustration and restlessness in the family's new furniture trade was not something that he could curb by keeping him in the workshop all day. He had sent Thomas to Matthew, to the farm he had inherited after his parents had moved into his married brother's *Dawdi* house. Uncle Jesse had believed that outdoor work would be the solution, although Matthew had not been so hopeful...

As the lane took them near to Lovina's family home, Matthew cleared his throat.

"I saw you talking to Tessa earlier," he said, nodding at the house ahead as though in reference.

"Nice girl," said Thomas, grinning.

"Yes, she is," said Matthew guardedly. "As his her sister."

"Lovina's a little old for me," teased Thomas, who had seen his cousin gazing at the eldest Lapp sister at social gatherings.

"You know I don't mean Lovina," said Matthew. "You were hanging around Verity the last two weeks, and it looked like you were interested in her."

"Did it now?" said Thomas.

"And she was obviously interested in you," said Matthew, risking the dangers of boosting Thomas' vanity in order to get to the point. "So what's she going to think if you transfer your affections to her sister?"

"Who says they've transferred?" laughed Thomas, taking a few longer strides which forced Matthew to hurry. He liked reminding Matthew of the four inch difference in their heights – a difference which Matthew, at twenty-two, was unlikely to recover.

"So you're not interested in Tessa?" pushed Matthew.

"Who says I have to pick one?" asked Thomas.

Matthew blinked. Then he felt his face grow warm. "Because otherwise you're just flirting with them."

"Oh, come on," said Thomas, still striding onward through the dusk. They had nearly drawn level with the Lapp home. "They know we're just having fun."

"Just... having fun?" Matthew repeated incredulously.

"Yes, fun, remember that, Matthew?"

Thomas laughed, and then waved – the Lapps had already reached their home, and the girls were on the porch. Tessa and Verity waved back. Matthew thought that he could see Lovina looking at him, though it was hard to tell given the distance and the darkness. He raised a hand, and she returned the gesture, but there was no hint of that earlier smile in her shadowed face.

***

"Maybe we should get married."

Lovina glanced up from the jacket in her lap. "Just cause I'm doing your mending doesn't mean I'm going to marry you, Matthew."

Matthew pulled a face at her, and she rolled her eyes.

It was only fair that she should fix it the jacket, Lovina decided. It was her fault, she had asked him to climb one of the beech trees and fetch a handful of the young, spring leaves, because her brother Zach had told her you could eat them.

Matthew had panicked when he had noticed the tear. Apparently, his mother had told him that the next time he ripped something, he would not be allowed go out and play for a whole month. Lovina did not know why Matthew's mother was so worried, as Matthew was already much more careful than the other boys – definitely more careful than her little brothers Zach, Jonathan and Henry. But Lovina did not want Matthew to get stuck indoors for a month, so she had volunteered to mend his jacket with the little sewing set she had been given three months earlier, just after her eighth birthday.

"Not cause of that," said Matthew, throwing a flower at her. He had been gathering them at the edge of the wood, near where Lovina was sitting. She secretly hoped he meant to give them to her, but did not want to ask.

"Why then?" she asked, holding the jacket to the light to see the stitching.

"Cause all the others are getting all worked up about it," he said. "As soon as they grow up, it's all they think about. You heard about Sadie and Isaac."

"It's not good to gossip."

"It's not gossip, everyone knows. She threw a rock at him."

"It was a pebble."

"Still." Matthew surveyed the bunch of flowers critically. "It's something they all worry about. If we decide now, we could forget about it til it comes up again."

"Maybe..." Lovina shook out the jacket. "There you go."

"Thank you," said Matthew again, and handed her the flowers he'd picked.

"I didn't say yes," joked Lovina, though she took the flowers anyway.

***

For Lovina, trying to catch all of her siblings in one place at one time was like trying to pick up water. They had their meals together, but the boys spent that time planning what they would be doing next on the farm, and Tessa and Verity talked... well, gossiped. Sometimes the boys ate before or after their sisters, fitting meals in around their work. Lovina knew that she should impress on them how important it was to spend time with their family, but she did not know how to go about it without seeming as though she was trying to make them feel guilty.

And now, when she had told all of them individually that she needed to speak to everyone in a group, they still could barely stop long enough to listen. Verity was already gone, having walked over to a friend's house as soon as she had done her chores, and Tessa was talking about her own plans for the day. And the boys looked like they were sleepwalking. They had been working too hard, again, and Lovina did not know how to get them to slow down.

"Wait, just wait," she called out, halting the boys on their way out of the door.

"We have to – " started Zach, as Jonathan rubbed his eyes blearily and Henry yawned.

"I know, just wait a moment – Tessa, hold on just a – "

"Sadie's expecting me, we're supposed to quilt – "

"I *know*," said Lovina, a little too loudly. Her siblings all looked at her then. None of them really looked the same as each other, with slightly varied hair colors, skin tones, and statures, but they all had their mother's bright hazel eyes. Their one link.

"You know it's the anniversary soon," she said, while she still had their attention. Their expressions immediately clouded over. "I was thinking we could do something, you know, like we used to. What do you think?"

There was a brief silence. "Sure," said Henry, glancing down. The others nodded.

"All right," said Lovina, heartened, "what should we do?"

They had used to picnic by the river, to remember the anniversary of their parents' deaths, but for the last two years everyone had decided that they were too busy to give up a whole afternoon.

"Whatever you want," said Zach, shrugging. The others were already turning to leave.

"But I – "

"We have to go."

"So do I," said Tessa, and she was out of the door before Lovina could get a word out.

Walking to the window, Lovina saw the tall, rangy figure of Thomas Zehr standing at her gate, waiting for her sister. As Tessa reached him, he bent down toward her, as though he were whispering something in her ear. Tessa laughed.

Lovina closed her eyes.

Lord, I don't know what to do. I was not old enough to become a mother to all of them, but they still needed one. I don't know how to reign in my sisters. I don't know how to stop my brothers working themselves to death, trying to live up to our father's name. I don't know how I could ever marry, and leave them, but I don't know how I can keep doing this without a partner to help me.

I don't know anything.

***

"Well, look at you!"

Matthew grinned at Lovina and stepped close to her, straightening up and judging the difference between his and Lovina's height with his hand.

"You're as tall as me!"

Lovina smiled at him. She had not seen him all Summer, as he had gone to stay with his aunt's family. He had a lot of family, but none of them ever came here, though she was not sure why. He was leaner and browner than he had been in the spring, and his nut-colored hair had been lightened in the sun, but he did not appear to have grown much. Still, he looked older. Lovina felt almost shy as she met his eyes.

"Maybe I'll overtake you," she said, falling into step with him as they began their old walk through the thick green shade under the beeches. "And you'll stay the same."

"Girls get taller quicker, everyone knows that," protested Matthew. "I'll have time to catch up, I'm not even twelve yet."

"Better hurry," laughed Lovina, standing on her toes to gain a couple more inches.

"Oh, I'm in no hurry to grow up." Matthew walked ahead a little.

Lovina felt there was an undercurrent to his words, but she could not place it.

"No?"

"No," repeated Matthew, his face set. Then he saw her looking at him and smiled. "Doesn't seem like a lot of fun, does it?"

"I don't know..." Lovina thought of her home, of how loving and warm it was, with her mother running everything with her capable hands and heart. "I'm looking forward to it."

"Not too soon though," said Matthew. He looked up at the canopy above them, grown thick and dense over so very many years.

***

Lovina could not believe what she was hearing. She looked at her sisters, both watching her with their eyebrows slightly raised, expressions that said clearly they were expecting her to make a scene. To pretend to be *Mamme*, whom she could never be. Lovina swallowed.

"Isn't this a little sudden?" she asked, trying to keep her voice quiet. Trying to remain reasonable.

Verity rolled her eyes, and Lovina felt a spark of temper which she quickly tamped down.

"We've been thinking about it for a while. We just decided. Why wait?"

"But why go away at all?" asked Lovina.

She had never even thought of going away for rumspringa when she was their age. Moving away from home, living somewhere else... not like others. She pushed the memory down.

But then, she had had her parents as her center. She had always known that she wanted to be in her home, and then to start her own home, building something that would last. She had had her mother to look up to. Verity and Tessa only had their failure of a big sister.

"How will you pay for everything?" she asked, trying to stick to simple points.

"We'll get jobs," said Tessa, as this were the most obvious thing in the world.

"Where?" asked Lovina. "And how?"

"Thomas said he knows – " started Tessa, before Verity elbowed her in the side.

But Lovina already felt something choking her.

"Thomas?" she said. "Thomas *Zehr*?" Neither of her sisters would meet her eyes across the kitchen table. "He's going on this – this trip as well, is he?" Lovina heard her voice becoming shrill.

"He was going on his own trip," corrected Verity in a sulky tone, "and said he could help us. He was being nice."

"Oh, very nice," said Lovina, pushing herself away from the table and heading out of the back door. She half-expected one of her sisters to call her back, but neither of them did.

She wandered across the pasture, half-blinded by the setting sun, until she reached the edge of the beech wood. Its deep, dark interior, shot through with golden flecks as the sun made its way between the branches, looked indescribably inviting.

But Lovina could not bring herself to enter it. If she and Matthew were still close – well, she would have gone to him now, that was certain.

She sank down into the grass, burying her fingers in the tufts of green.

Lord. If they have to leave – if I have to let them go – I understand. But why must it break my heart?

If I am meant to be alone –

The thoughts stopped Lovina in her tracks for a moment and she had to take a deep breath before she continued her prayer.

– Then let me rejoice in it, Lord. Let me be as one of the apostles who found their family in the church, who did not need children, or siblings, or marriage. Please, Lord, if I am not to have these things, let me not want them any more.

Lovina sat quietly, waiting. Waiting to stop wanting. Waiting for her heart to let go of the dreams she kept coming back to. But nothing happened.

***

"How is he?"

Lovina shook her head. "They've given him orders to rest, but that's still no guarantee that it won't happen again, or that it won't get worse."

Matthew bit his lip. Lovina's father had been complaining of shortness of breath and dizzy spells for a while now, and a week ago he had passed out in the fields. It seemed strange to see Lovina looking like this, so pale and exhausted, with the appearance of someone far older than her thirteen years.

"How are your brothers and sisters?" he asked. "I guess Tessa and Verity must be taking this hard."

Lovina's sisters had always been a little too sensitive. High-strung, Lovina's mother called it. He had grown to know them well over the years, through his friendship with Lovina, and he felt strangely guilty at the fact that he could do nothing to protect them from what they were going through. Not that he did not want to protect Lovina as well, but she had been oddly withdrawn over the past week. She had been busy, of course, helping her mother run things. But Matthew had not been able to speak to her before the walk they were taking today.

And now that they were in their special place, under the beech trees – even though the branches were barren, forming cracks against the hard winter sky, the place was still a comfort – he did not feel as though he could burden her with his own problems.

As though she could tell what he was thinking, Lovina turned to him.

"What about you?" she asked. "How have you been since I saw you last, how's your family?"

Matthew opened his mouth to tell her.

Then closed it.

"Fine," he said. "Same as normal."

Well, that was the truth.

"Good," said Lovina, "that's... that's good..." her voice caught, and her face crumpled.

Matthew stood awkwardly as Lovina turned away to cry. He knew that she would be embarrassed about him seeing her like this, but he could hardly pretend that it was not happening.

"I'm fine," mumbled Lovina, burying her face in her handkerchief.

"I can tell," said Matthew, which at least made her laugh.

"I'm sorry," she said, wiping at her eyes. "I just – there's just so much, suddenly. My brothers and sisters, and my parents, they're all relying on me, and I don't know if I can handle everything."

"You can," said Matthew.

Lovina gave him a half, somewhat watered-down smile.

"And if you ever can't," he continued, "if it's ever too much, if something happens that your parents can't help you with, you just come and find me. I'll be there."

Lovina looked at him for a long moment. "Promise?" she said.

***

Matthew had decided, before beginning this conversation, that he was going to keep his temper. Amazingly, he had managed to do so.

What he had not counted on, however, was Thomas being unable to keep his.

"Why can't you leave me alone?" the younger man demanded, eyes narrow and hard. "What's it got to do with you?"

"It's inappropriate," said Matthew, his tone even. "You've been flirting with both of them, openly, and – "

"And all the old folks will talk, I know, how terrible. You're worried people are going to think you were a bad influence on me?"

Matthew counted to ten inside his head before speaking. He looked at the clock on the wall of the living room so that he would not be tempted to rush.

"Won't you think of the girls, then?" he asked. "Tessa and Verity might end up with damaged reputations if you keep on as you are."

"It's not my fault if people gossip," said Thomas, his cheeks staining red. "We haven't done anything wrong, Matthew. I've never touched either of them."

"But how have you been looking at them, Thomas?" Matthew asked quietly. "Where do your thoughts about them lead you?"

Thomas broke eye contact, scowling at his feet.

"You really think I'm worried about other people's opinions?" said Matthew. "God's opinion is the only one that matters." Thomas remained silent, so Matthew tried another push. "You know that I'm the last person who could judge you – "

But at this, Thomas' head shot up. "Yes," he said, "You are the last person who could judge me. In fact, I thought you all of all people would understand, but you're just as self-righteous as the rest of them."

He pushed himself out of his chair and headed for the door.

Matthew stood and followed him to the porch, more to see where he was going than to try and start the conversation over. There would be chance for that later, when Thomas had calmed down. But as he watched Thomas heading with angry steps out into the fields, his attention was suddenly drawn by a figure standing nearer to him. At the gate – just outside the gate, looking at the house as though wondering whether to approach.

"Lovina?"

Matthew walked across the yard to her as she made her way to him, so that they met at the center. It was early evening, and the air was cool and fresh after a shower of rain a few hours before. The cloud cover had broken into large, fluffy mounds, with starkly sunlit outlines. Lovina stood in the pearly light, her face serious.

"Did Thomas tell you?" she asked. "Is that what you were arguing about?"

"You heard that?"

"I heard him yelling."

"Oh – wait." Matthew paused, frowning. "Did he tell me about what?"

Lovina broke the news to him about the plan which her sisters had let slip. As he listened, Matthew felt a surge of protection for Tessa and Verity. He had never been able to shake the feeling that they should by rights have been a part of his family, even though the hopes of that becoming a reality had long been lost.

"Thank you for telling me this," he said as she finished. "I suppose... I suppose I can send Thomas back to his parents."

"They could still meet up, if they all leave," said Lovina, shaking her head. She reached up and pinched the bridge of her nose, an action that seemed to belong to someone far older than she was.

"You can't convince the girls to stay?" asked Matthew.

He regretted the question as Lovina met his eyes with a burning gaze.

"*No,*" she said. "I can't. I can't make them do anything. *I'm not my mother.*"

"No one's expecting you to be your mother," Matthew said gently.

"Aren't they?" Lovina snapped. "No, no, I guess they're not, because even my mother couldn't handle everything herself, she had my father. I don't understand – "

She pinched the bridge of her nose once more, and Matthew barely heard the words that came next:

"I don't understand why I have to do this alone."

"You're not alone," he said, "I'm – " and then he stopped, realizing how similar this was to another conversation they had once had.

From the way she was watching him, Lovina had clearly made the connection as well.

" – I'm here," he finished. Because he had to.

Lovina looked at him a moment longer, then dipped her head in a nod, her mouth pressed together.

"Lovina," said Matthew, "it's not the same as it was. I'm not the same."

"Neither am I," she said.

***

"You're really going."

They had come to say goodbye, under the beech trees. Matthew had bid the Lapps a polite family farewell, but Lovina had known, somehow, that he would be waiting for her here.

Lovina was aware that she had not spoken to Matthew, not properly, in a long time. Wrapped up in her family, she had hardly had the chance, or that is what she told herself. She knew that things at his home had not been good for a long time – if ever they had been good – but she had not expected this.

He was leaving. Going away, for Rumspringa. He was getting a job somewhere, with the intention of traveling around as much of the country as he could see.

"You'll be all right," he said.

Lovina's father had not had a bad spell for a year, though he had never regained his full strength. He was training the boys to run the farm, and they had thrown themselves into it as though they could bring him back to life as they brought life from the soil.

"What about you?" she asked.

"Don't worry about me." His voice was flat and removed, as though he were saying the words by rote. As though there was no reason to think that she actually would worry about him.

When was the last time anybody worried about you, she wondered, as she watched her childhood friend turn and walk away into something he hoped would become freedom.

***

It had been hard enough to get the three of them to agree to this; Matthew had hoped that they would at least take it seriously. But Thomas was leaning his elbows on the table with an indolent air, and Tessa and Verity kept exchanging glances and smirking.

Well, there was nothing for it.

"Lovina told me what you're planning," he started.

"Why do I feel like I'm back at school...?" murmured Thomas, and the girls spluttered with laughter.

Matthew gritted his teeth for a moment. He wondered if he should have remained standing, rather than sitting opposite them.

"You know that I did something similar myself," he said.

"We know," said Tessa. "You had all of your fun, and then decided to come back and be good."

"And now you think that we should make the same decision as you, with none of the fun," said Thomas.

Matthew took a long, deep breath. He leaned back a little, and looked up at the ceiling.

"Maybe I should just let you go," he said quietly – so quietly, that he sensed the others were having to pay real attention to listen in. "But if my experiences could help someone else, then maybe they'd be worth something. Maybe some good could come out of it all."

He looked back at the three before him.

"Rumspringa can be an opportunity," he said. "For some, it is a chance to find out what it really means to make a commitment. Others find that they might be called to live a different life. Some just need to get perspective. And if I felt that your plan involved any one of these, I wouldn't say a word."

He felt his gaze harden, and a sternness crept into his voice.

"But this, what you want," he said, "is pleasure. Worldly pleasure. You don't want to try a different perspective, or build something new. You want to break all the rules you have had to live with, and forget the consequences."

Thomas opened his mouth to speak, but Matthew held up his hand.

"But what you don't know – and it is a privilege not to know this, believe me – is that there are consequences. Real dangers, and in the lifestyle you're headed toward, you're going to find them as soon as you get there."

There was a moment's silence. Verity traced a pattern on the tabletop with her finger.

"So there's a danger," she said. "But won't it be worth it? For freedom?"

You don't want freedom, thought Matthew. *You want to escape a home that is not the one you grew up so loved and coddled in, and a life that you don't want to face.*

But that was not what she needed to hear right now.

"They didn't call it freedom," he said. "The people I met. They called it something else."

He had hoped never to remember this.

"They called it oblivion." He closed his eyes. "*Total oblivion.*"

He knew, from the hush on the other side of the table, that he finally had their complete attention.

So he told them. He told of the oblivion he had found, and the people he had found it with. People who had emptiness behind their eyes, and teeth instead of smiles, whose minds had not been their own in years. Rooms that existed only in darkness, people whose lives centered only on the things that happened in those rooms. Relationships that had seemed like they meant something, only to twist themselves into nothingness. The degradation, the hopelessness of it all, the way you became bound to your body as though you were its slave, allowed only to bring it what it demanded, feeding appetites which only seemed to grow.

He told them, and they listened.

***

"Matthew?"

Matthew could not understand what he was looking at. Was it the ocean? It kept moving, he could hear it, and it was a greeny-gray color. But it was so far away. It made him feel happy. Like everything was going to be all right. And that voice, too, that made him happy.

"Matthew, I've called the boys, they're going to take you to your aunt's, I don't think you should go home like this."

Matthew felt his thoughts slowly coming back to his head. He opened his eyes all the way. Oh, right, that wasn't the sea. It was the canopy of the beech wood, and he was lying beneath it on his back.

And there was Lovina, looking at him.

Wait – Lovina?

She looked the same. Different. Older.

Matthew tried to push himself up, but Lovina was already kneeling beside him, telling him to stay still.

"You look like you'll snap in half if you try to move," she said, her voice soft.

Matthew frowned, wondering what she meant. He tried to think of what he looked like... when was the last time he had seen his reflection? He had a dim memory of a mirror in a grimy gas station bathroom, seen sometime in the last couple of days. His skin had been pale, faintly jaundiced, stretched paper thin over jutting bones. The florescent light had cast shadows in his eyes and in the hollows of this cheeks.

"How did you even get here?" he heard Lovina murmur.

"Walked," he told her. Obviously. And he smiled, because even though she had tears in her eyes, it was Lovina, and they were in the beech wood, exactly where they should be.

"My parents..." he started to say, trying to sit again.

With a gentle touch to his shoulder, Lovina pushed him down. He noticed one of his sleeves sliding up, and hastily pulled the cuff back to his wrist.

"You can go to them once you're well," said Lovina. "I think it will be all right. They've been doing better, these past couple of years. I think you leaving shook them. They've been getting help from the preachers. Counseling."

"Right. Good for them," said Matthew, smiling wryly. Yes, good for them, how nice for them. "And your parents?" he asked.

There was a pause, during which all he could hear was the swishing and hissing of leaves in the wind.

"They're dead, Matthew," said Lovina.

The words took a few moments to penetrate.

"What."

"Two years ago, a few months after you left."

Matthew shook his head. "But – no – "

"*Mamme* got sick," said Lovina. "It was sudden. When he knew she wasn't going to make it, *Daed* just gave up. They went the same night."

"No – "

This was wrong. This was not supposed to happen. He had said, he had promised –

"I said I would be here," he whispered. "I said I would be here for you."

"Yes," said Lovina. "You did say that."

And Lovina was standing, moving away from him, creating a distance between them that he would never have a right to recover.

***

He works all things together for the good.

Lovina was not sure why this verse had been buzzing around her head all morning. She had been praying as she completed her chores, and it had popped into her mind. And stayed there. Almost as though it were being said to her, over and over...

All things together for the good of those who love him.

And then, as she heard the door to the kitchen open and close, *his plans are better than yours.*

She turned, and saw Tessa and Verity. Their eyes were reddened and swollen.

Lovina nearly dropped the bowl she was holding. She could not remember the last time either of them had cried.

"What happened? What's wrong?"

"Nothing," said Verity, shaking her head. "Nothing's wrong."

***

"Thought I'd find you here."

Lovina stopped walking and turned, waiting for Matthew to catch her up. It was midday, and by rights she should have been attending to her work, but she had felt the cool green of the beech wood calling to her, for the first time in years. She had left Verity and Tessa in charge, and escaped to the shade of the canopy. The two of them had been in a whirl of baking, preparing for the picnic they were determined to have the next day, just as they used to, to remember their parents.

"Have you spoken to the girls?" asked Matthew, falling into easy step next to her. They always walked at the same pace, Lovina remembered, being the exact same height.

"They didn't want to talk too much yesterday," said Lovina, "but they told me what you'd... discussed."

"Ah."

"Thank you. For telling them. That must have been difficult."

Matthew shrugged. "It was necessary," he said, but his tone betrayed how hard he had found it. "Are they staying, then?" he asked.

"Verity is," said Lovina. "Tessa still wants to go away for a while, but she's talking about getting a real job, and we've discussed things like a self-imposed curfew, keeping in touch... she's trying to be responsible."

Matthew nodded. "Thomas is saying something similar," he said. "Though, to be honest, I get the feeling that he's not going to see it through."

"No?"

"No, I think he was just getting carried away with the idea of *no rules*. I told him to pray about it – maybe he'll still go, but I think it's going to be all right either way."

"I think you scared them straight," said Lovina, trying to be a little flippant, but Matthew's face creased.

"I'm sorry if any of it was too upsetting," he said. "I don't know how much they told you – "

"I'd guessed most of it," said Lovina. "You said some things, that day I found you here."

"I did?" Matthew ran a hand over his head and rubbed the back of his neck. "I'm sorry."

"It's all right."

"No, really, I'm sorry, for everything, Lovina." He stopped walking, his face earnest.

Lovina stopped too and shook her head, indicating that he did not need to continue, but he pressed on.

"I wasn't here," he said, "when you needed me. I let you down. I'm sorry."

He was standing close, so close, his expression open, and Lovina felt the bond between them as roots beneath the surface of the earth. Hidden, buried, never gone.

"I let you down first," she said. Because it was the truth. "You needed me, and I left you alone."

Matthew looked as though he wanted to argue, but Lovina met his gaze straight on and he hesitated. She knew that he knew she was right.

"Well, then," he said slowly. "Perhaps we should agree that we won't leave each other again."

Lovina felt a smile being pulled to the surface, as though her happiness were seeking fresh air and sunshine.

"Never again," she agreed.

And they walked on, through the warm green light that filtered down through the beech leaves.

LOVINA

Lovina rolled over in her cotton sheets and stared out the window at the sun beaming through the ragged curtains of her bedroom. The light from the morning lit up the interior of her modest room. The cock crowed as she stirred and stepped from the comfort of the warm bed. As her delicate toes touched the floor she winced at the feel of the cool floorboards beneath her feet. She mentally prepared herself for another typical day in the remote Amish community where she was raised. She sat on the edge of her bed and began braiding her long, golden locks. Her hair had never been cut. Once finished she tied a tiny, white bow at the end. Standing up, her hair extended all the way down to her upper thighs.

From the homely bedside table, she grabbed her prayer cap, the white cap made of organza and stiff with starch that she must wear in public. She slipped it over her long, golden braid and stood, making her way over to the wardrobe, barefoot. The floorboards creaked beneath her slender frame. The house in which she lived was in need of much repair, but it was home.

Her dress was bound by the Amish community to which she belonged. She pulled out the calf-length, gray dress, and her white apron to accompany it. She looked the outfit up and down, sighing at the restrictions she had to abide by. Just a little color or a little lace would make it so much more tolerable, but alas it was forbidden.

She slipped the dress over her head, atop the white, cotton undergarments she wore beneath. Her slender arms penetrated the long sleeves at the ends and her delicate fingers stretched out toward the floor. Her blue eyes reflected in the full-length mirror that stood opposite. They ran over her entire frame, assessing the modesty of her attire. Her smooth legs peeked out the bottom of the gown. Her hands just protruded from the sleeves. How she longed for something different. To have somewhat more choice when it came to the little things. But living here her options were overly restricted. With a sigh, she turned away from her dull reflection.

Her stomach growled lightly, alerting her that breakfast time was upon her. Before leaving, she quickly raced to the window and opened it wide, allowing the cool morning air to hit her face. It almost stung as the contrasting wind nipped at her warm skin. She turned on her heels and made her way to the exit of her humble sanctuary, ready to start the day ahead.

Before opening the door she took a deep breath, hearing the faint clip-clop of hooves outside. She felt a tear well up in the corner of her eye, but she willed it to stop. No matter how much she tried, Lovina was overwhelmed with pain with any reminder of her parent's accident. No day since their passing had her parent's death become any easier for Lovina. Each day she was reminded of the terrible accident they had undertaken. As soon as she set eyes on the cart outside, laying rusted and disheveled. Unused for a year. A constant visual scar, sitting in their front yard. Although she knew that her brother, Jacob, shared her pain she would not dare discuss with him.

He had been walking down the street when it occurred. On his way back from the cornfields down the road from their home. Their mother and father waved as they passed, smiling at him. The next thing Jacob knew, he was watching their cart overturn as the horses bucked and bolted, leaving the two bodies trapped beneath the wreckage. Around him, people screamed at the sight, but all he could do was rush over to find his parents laying lifeless in the middle of the dirt road.

Lovina was distraught. She cried for weeks. She took to her room and moped. No one could comfort her. Since then the community had done their best to assist the two orphaned children. They stayed in the family home, but here they could barely make ends meet. Her job as a milkmaid at the dairy farm and his as an apprentice blacksmith left them living pay day to pay day. They relied on handouts from neighbors and friends to feed themselves. Still, Lovina and Jacob vowed to take care of themselves, and that was just what they did. Regardless of if it was against the rules.

One evening, months after the accident, Jacob had an idea. He weighed it up in his mind over and over. He had promised Lovina the day of their parents passing that he would always take care of her. That was just what he intended to do. But not if it meant risking her safety or standing within the community. Finally, he decided that there was no other option for them. The need for financial stability was too great.

"Come out with me tonight," he had asked, his voice trembling with what she felt to be nerves, excitement or worry, she could not distinguish.

"To where?" she had asked, but he would not answer. Lovina was wary at first of her brother's sudden plan. Still, she trusted him and so she followed, through the woods and to the city on the other side.

"Where are we going, Jacob?" she asked on their journey. He turned and held out his hand, signaling her to stop in her tracks. He opened the knapsack he had been holding tightly to his chest since they had left the community. Inside was a range of colorful clothing, the likes of which Lovina had never seen.

"I am taking you to the city," he explained, pulling out a pale pink fitted dress and white heels for his sister. She stared in awe at the strange fabric garments handed to her.

"You need to wear these, otherwise they will know we are not from there," he explained. Entering a modern city in their modest attire would surely give them away as patrons of the well-known Amish district just miles away. Jacob had experienced this prejudice first hand after all.

"I will stand over there. Let me know when you have changed. You can put your clothes in this bag," he gestured to the bag from which he had pulled the new outfit. Then he turned and walked out of sight, giving his sister the privacy to change.

She untied her apron and dropped her dress to the forest floor. She folded them and placed them in the knapsack Jacob had provided. She shivered in the cold night air. Picking up the new dress she pulled it gingerly over her head. It was so tight and firm around her body. She looked down at herself in the odd creation. Quickly she slipped the heels on her feet and called out,

"I think I am ready Jacob!" moments later he emerged from the shadows. He paused, taken aback by his sister's speedy transformation. He took her hand and kicked the knapsack into a large bush beside them.

"Time to go then," he whispered and they were off again through the trees.

When they came out on the other side of the vast wood, Lovina stopped in awe. The lights glistened in the distance as they looked over the high-rise jungle. Jacob had been lucky enough to experience life on the other side. This is where he had been during Rumspringa, but his freedom was short-lived. He promptly returned to the community, overwhelmed by the progression he experienced.

Lovina had not had that luxury. This was her first time in the city, even seeing it from a distance.

"Why are you bringing me here?" she mumbled. Jacob's expression became serious.

"We need money, Lovina. I did not want to worry you with such matters but since our parents passing we have been struggling... more than you know." she had no idea what this had to do with going to the city.

"We can get jobs here. Second jobs, at night. It has been so hard for us Annaliese and I need your help. Please," he begged. But she would do anything for her brother. She took his hand once more and squeezed it kindly.

"Then let's go," she said, excitedly.

Months later and they had been working at the diner quite regularly, almost every night. Lovina darted around in her short, yellow waitressing uniform, serving tables left and right. After her first day, she was amazed at how much money she had made, and just in tips. In the kitchen her brother worked hastily, cleaning dish after dish and piles of cutlery. But neither of them minded the hard work, especially Lovina. She was happy to just be out in the real world.

"Order up!" the chef boomed from the service window. He rang the bell relentlessly to alert her of food being ready to pick up. She scooted over and took it to her waiting customers. Now she had everything down to a fine art.

The sneaking around was getting quite cumbersome, however. Her heart raced each night her and Jacob ventured out, against the communities wishes. That night when she got home she collapsed on the bed and stared up at the ceiling. Exhausted, she wished her life was more simple. Leading her dual existence was taking its toll on her. She was plagued with a lack of sleep and a crippling anxiety. Tossing and turning during her few hours sleep each night. Alas, she had no other choice, for now anyway. She felt a huge debt weighing on her, for her brother. He had taken care of Lovina since their parent's sudden demise. No matter how much she wished she could leave, it was not an option.

One morning as she was walking down the street, Lovina was greeted by an unexpected face.

"Lovina!" a man's voice boomed from behind her. She turned quickly on her heel to see an old friend, one whom she thought had left for good years earlier.

"Jebidiah?" she said, stunned. Her grocery basket fell to the ground with a thud as she ran toward him and wrapped her arms around his broad shoulders. He picked her up around the waist and they held their embrace for several seconds. Even though it had been so long since their last encounter, neither failed to recognize the other.

He dropped her back to the ground and she stepped back slightly to take in the sight of her long lost friend. His hair was styled just as it always had been. His dark brown locks were cut short, a few inches from his scalp. It hung in waves around his face. His skin was tanned and contrasted perfectly with his strong, masculine jawline and muscular figure. His chin was littered with stubble, giving his face a slight shadowing.

Their last meeting had not been so joyous. Jebidiah had been leaving for Rumspringa with her brother Jacob. The three children had grown up as close as they could be, spending endless hours together playing in the cornfields and chasing each other through the streets. Since the age of five, Lovina and Jebidiah had known each other. She saw him as one of her closest friends. Or at least she had before he disappeared.

It had been a cold night, pelting down with rain. They stood there, facing each other. Lovina had been fifteen, Jebidiah sixteen. Not a word was spoken for several minutes between them. Too young to realize the deep feelings that connected them, Jebidiah left with Jacob, to experience the modern world with the rest of the community boys coming of age that year. Lovina had waited for him. She waited up at night and watched for him during the day. But he did not return.

Jacob came back weeks later with a few of the neighborhood boys, but Jebidiah was not among them.

Her brother had rested his hand on her shoulder as tears rolled down her face, tears for the loss of her best friend.

"He said to tell you he will see you again. He promised." at the time Lovina had not believed him. She had thought her brother was trying desperately to bring her out of her deepening hole of overwhelming sadness. But with Jebidiah standing before her, Jacob's words echoed in the midst of her thoughts.

'He promised.'

She had given up hope of seeing him again, yet here he stood, in the flesh.

Jebidiah was speechless. He had returned to the community after years. It seemed that no matter how much the modern world drew him, his love for Lovina was stronger. From the day he had left, he did not stop thinking about her, not for a moment. It had been fun and he savored the new experiences put forth by his peers in the city, but no one could replace her. That was what influenced him to return. There was nothing more he could gain from the city, he was looking to start a family. Jebidiah could not consider anyone else he would rather make a life with than her.

"I hope Jacob gave you my message all those years ago," he said, smiling down at her from above.

"He did," she replied, mirroring the beam that had taken over Jebidiah's face. Any onlooker could tell that these two were much more than just friends, even if they had not yet admitted it to themselves. They still grasped the hands of each other as they chatted for a few minutes about shared memories from the past.

Jebidiah bent down and picked up the discarded basket of groceries Lovina had dropped in her shock at his appearance.

"Let's go for a walk, I need to catch up with you. So much has happened in the last few years I am sure," he laughed. As they strolled along they spoke at length about their experiences. Everything Jebidiah said about his time away absolutely intrigued her. She desperately wished that she could share in this modern world, if only for a day. Working was all she had ever had the chance to do when her and Jacob managed to escape for their night shifts.

"So, what about your life, Lovina?" he questioned. After a moment of thought, he saw her face drop. The only significant thing she could think of to tell him was of her parent's sudden demise the previous fall. She took a deep breath and prepared herself for the retelling of the most painful memory she possessed.

"Actually, there was an accident last year," she began. Jebidiah's permanent grin faded almost immediately.

"My parents cart overturned. It was terrifying but the worst was that they did not make it." Jebidiah could not find the words to express his condolences. After a few moments to comprehend the brief and saddening story he mustered,

"I am so sorry, Lovina."

As always, her first thought was to change the subject, and so she did. Long ago she had decided that her parents would not have wanted her to mourn, but cherish the life that she had. That was exactly what she intended to do. The sadness they had been wallowing in for that brief moment evaporated quickly as they moved on to more trivial and light-hearted news from their vast time apart.

Jebidiah walked her all the way back to her door. He handed back the basket as she stepped through the threshold of the dark, polished doorway.

"Well, I am sure we will see each other again soon," he said as he turned to leave.

"You will," she smiled and with that the door clicked shut behind her.

As the following months flew by, Lovina found herself spending more and more of her limited free time with her long lost friend. Jebidiah found comfort in their closeness. Since moving back, he had faced endless scrutiny from the older members of the place he called home. They frowned upon him for his rash decision to leave, now that he had returned. He had known upon his abrupt return to his family that not everyone would be so welcoming. But no one else mattered as long as Lovina was by his side.

She found comfort in his company too. She was intrigued by his endless stories of the new technologies and strange architecture he had encountered in his years away. Unlike her peers, Lovina held nothing against him for leaving, if anything she wished that she could do the same.

The two companions spent their time just as they did, years earlier. Exploring the now familiar woods. Chasing each other through the cornfields. Collapsing with laughter on the dirt floor of the outdoors. They savored each moment they spent in each others company. To Lovina, no one could compare to Jebidiah.

One sunny afternoon, they fell into each other's arms in the dewy grass of the outskirts of the boundary. Their laughter subsided and

Lovina looked up at Jebidiah, beaming down at her. She knew that there was something deeper. This was not just another friendship, he meant so much more. Every second without him left her feeling cold and empty. Every second without her made him feel as if he was completely alone.

"Do you think you will stay here this time?" Lovina asked. She hoped that his answer reflected the way that she felt. But alas, he uttered the answer she did not want to hear.

"No. I think that now I have experienced what is out there, lived my life outside the confines of the community, I don't want to leave again." her heart dropped. There was nothing in the world she wished for more than to go, but a life without Jebidiah seemed just as empty.

It was his strength that encouraged her to plan her escape, to a new life in the modern world. Deep in her heart she knew that it was unlikely Jebidiah would come with her. After all, he had returned not weeks ago, but she had to follow her dreams. She had but one life, and she intended to live it. As much as she wanted to share with him her wishes, she knew this was one secret she must keep to herself.

Jebidiah walked her home again that day, as he often did of late. The sun was setting over the sovereign hills as they strolled past people and places on the way home. She took in the sights, for in a few weeks they would be gone forever. There was no doubt she would miss this place, but most of all she would miss him. She cherished the time they had together, though short lived.

They arrived at her home. Before she opened the door, Jebidiah grasped her wrist tightly. Her skin broke out in goosebumps all over in response to his flesh against hers. Her heart raced within her chest cavity. Cheeks began to glow red as the blood from her pounding heart rushed to her face. She hoped that Jebidiah did not see the intense reaction she gave from his touch.

"Do you have plans for tomorrow?" he questioned. His expression was serious all of a sudden.

"No," Lovina responded. Where was he going with this?

"I see, well goodnight then," he said with a grin. How strange. With that Jebidiah let go of her arm and placed his hands into his pockets.

"Goodbye," she called to him as he strolled slowly away, toward his family home at the end of the road.

As she closed the door behind her Lovina leaned her back against the rough wood and closed her eyes. The overwhelming sensation of lust she felt for Jebidiah was quickly blooming into a raging passion. Love. Little did she know that he felt it too. From the top of her head to the far tips of her toes her entire being was filled with admiration and desire for him. How would she tell him that she was going to leave the town? Start a new life in the place that he had run from.

She already had a plan in place. Two weeks from now she would be living amongst the modern world. Jacob had not been pleased, but he knew that he could not stop his sister from following her dreams. He had the opportunity, so there was no way that he could deny her that right, regardless of the community law.

"Are you sure you will be OK on your own?" Jacob could not hide the worried tone of his voice. Not even he could brave the new world, how could his little sister live there alone?

"I will, please do not worry about me, Jacob," then she explained her plan.

In the dead of night, while the town slept, she would sneak silently through the streets. Toward the wood. The path that they had traveled hundreds of times before would lead her to her new existence. She could not leave during the day, for fear of what scrutiny she may face from the others in the town. Women rarely left and were never welcomed home. It was best for her to just disappear.

"But you have never been that way alone." he said, his voice still trembling with fear for Lovina.

"I have mapped out our way. The last few weeks I have made a note of each landmark along the path. Each time I feel as if my feet lead me more and more. I step without hesitation." slowly she had memorized the way. Every rock and tree, branch and shrub. The dirt clearings and the overgrown mangling of tangled weeds, she was confident in her navigational ability. Even if Jacob was not so.

"Where will you stay?" his questions kept coming. But Lovina was not one to take her decisions lightly. To his every question, she had the perfect answer. During their time at the diner, they had made a few friends, both co-workers, and customers. Lovina had organized a room in a modest apartment with Katie, a fellow waitress at a neighboring restaurant. For only a small portion of her minimum wage, she had a place to her her own.

Several hours later, Lovina had assured her brother that she could fend for herself. If she ever needed him, he would be there for her too.

Jacob took her hand and looked at her, eyes full of sadness.

"I will always be here for you, sister," a single tear rolled down his cheek, winding its way through the stubble on his strong chin. Lovina was taken aback, she had not seen her brother so emotional since their parents passing. She whispered the only words that came to mind in response to his heartfelt confession.

"I know," tears now flowed freely down their faces. They sat in silence as Jacob took in the news she had revealed to him. The plan she had derived. How much he would miss her.

The hardest part was over. Lovina had dreaded telling her brother about her escape. Now she felt free, with his blessing she could leave without hesitation. She slept that night, soundly for the first time in many moons. Dreaming of the future adventures she would have in the big city.

The next morning Jebidiah was at her door before either of the siblings had risen. She heard the light tapping from her bedroom and quickly dressed to see who was so desperate to see them this day. She raced down the creaking steps and to the front door. Opening it widely she was ecstatic to see Jebidiah standing there with a bouquet of red roses. Their scent was swept immediately into her nostrils and she closed her eyes as the aroma intoxicated her.

"Good morning, Lovina," Jebidiah greeted her, placing the stunning bunch into her hands.

"Hello," she replied, staring at the gift he had brought for her. Something was different about him this morning. She could not pick it but his smile was strange somehow, brighter than she had seen before. His eyes sparkled in the morning light. Her heart skipped a beat as they paused for a moment, looking deeply into each other's eyes.

"I have a day planned for us," he said excitedly. Before she had time to properly lace up her boots, Jebidiah took her hand and whisked her away from her home. They walked together toward the vast cornfields at the end of the street. Waving at their fellow community members as they passed, Jebidiah led Lovina through the tall corn stalks.

She had no idea what he had in store. They rushed forward in silence. Lovina found her mind wandering as she took in the rays of sunlight winding through the stalks and leaves surrounding them. Her dress occasionally caught on rouge sticks and branches strewn throughout the fields. She stumbled a few times, but Jebidiah was there to catch her and help her find her feet once more.

Minutes passed and they finally arrived at the small clearing in the far end of the fields. Jebidiah let her hand drop and pulled a blanket from the backpack he had been lugging with them on the short journey. He laid it delicately out on the ground, straightening the edges and patting it down flat.

"Come, sit," he gestured to a soft spot on the blanket and she slowly approached, sitting down carefully, holding her dress flat against her thighs as she lowered her body to the ground. She watched on as Jebidiah began unpacking a picnic that he had prepared. She was stunned at the romantic setting that he had created for just the two of them, out of nowhere.

"I hope you're hungry," he laughed. Her eyes drifted from plate to plate, each piled high with sandwiches and cakes, fruit and salads. She could not believe what she saw before her. This was the kind of thing she had always dreamed of but had never eventuated into a reality. The sun beamed down on them as they began their conversations.

"Please," Jebidiah picked up a plate of her favorite sandwiches, fresh strawberry jam. She picked up one and took a bite. The sweetness of the jam found every corner of her tongue, leaving a lasting sensation in her mouth as she swallowed. He watched her intently, looking as if something was weighing heavily on his mind. Lovina looked into his deep, brown eyes. She felt herself smile as she took in his handsome features, just inches from her. His short, dark hair flowed subtly in the mild breeze. Her gaze followed his masculine jawline and rugged chin, covered in light stubble.

It was at that moment Jebidiah uttered the words she had been longing for him to say for so long,

"I love you, Lovina, I always have." she was taken aback. Of course, her heart reciprocated his feelings, but she could not bring herself to say the words back. In the back of her mind, she knew that if she revealed her love for him she must also let him in on the fact she was planning to leave. Leave him and everything else behind. Moments later she found her voice once more,

"I love you too."

They spoke for hours after Jebidiah's unexpected, but heartfelt, confession. Of life and the paths they wanted to take in the future. That was when troubles arose.

"I just want to settle down, and have a family. I love it so much here. It feels so right to be back." Jebidiah said in between bites of his rosy red apple. Lovina froze. This was exactly the life she was running from. It was the first time that she realized that their journeys may lead them in different directions. She sat silent for a moment as he waited patiently for her to say something, anything. She took a deep breath and proceeded to reveal her underlying plan to Jebidiah. Her plan to leave and start a new life in the city he had fled from.

"I had no idea," Jebidiah gasped, in response to her and Jacob's secret second existence outside of the community. His heart dropped as she continued to explain her plans to escape and live amongst the modern world. Never had he thought coming into the fields with her that morning that she would drop this bombshell upon him. All hopes of his quiet life back at home with his childhood sweetheart were slowly evaporating before his eyes.

"When do you plan to leave?" he questioned, his heartbeat pounding in his chest. He prayed that it was not soon. That he would have time to change her mind.

"Two weeks from today," she admitted. His smile had faded, and hers with it. She had thought that the hardest conversation before her departure was over, but she had not counted on Jebidiah's romantic notions. His proposal of a simple, family life in the mundane town she had always lived. She loved him deeply, but her want for adventure was overwhelming.

With the sun beginning to lower over the tips of the corn, they decided that it was time to return. She folded the blanket as Jebidiah picked up the empty plates that surrounded them in the clearing. He took her hand and led the way back through the towering stalks. They moved at a much slower pace upon their return. Lovina could not be sure, maybe it was due to the dimming light, but she felt as if their lagging pace was a bi-product of the conversations they had just had. Of her leaving him and the rest of her life behind.

Eventually, they reached her front door once more. She stepped up the front stair and peered down at him.

"Thank you for today, Jebidiah. I had an amazing time. I really appreciate all that you have done for me," Lovina checked quickly for onlookers and before a word could escape his lips she kissed him tenderly on the cheek. By the time Jebidiah realized what had happened she had already stepped back inside.

He began his journey home, filled with mixed emotions from the day just passed. He desperately wanted Lovina to stay, but he understood her position was difficult. With constant reminders daily of her parent's death, he could only imagine the heartache she must feel living here.

Two weeks later, the grandfather clock below the stairs began chiming midnight. Lovina knew this was her chance to make her escape quietly, without fear of waking her sleeping neighborhood. She tiptoed down the stairs, their echoing creaks masked by the gongs of the great timekeeper. Her blonde locks fell over her face as she looked down toward the door, her destination on this dark winter night. She brushed them aside and kept moving. Grabbing the already assembled knapsack from its hiding spot, she slipped her pale pink coat over her slender shoulders and on the final stroke of midnight the door clicked shut behind her.

The cool wind bit at her exposed flesh as she crept through the dead of night. She knew that by leaving she was breaking her oath to the Church, but the call of the outside world was just too great. Not even her one true love could keep her from following her dreams. A single tear rolled slowly down her pale cheek as she looked back, back at the friends and family she would no longer see. Back at Jebidiah.

Tearing her gaze away she strove forward. Her hair was now wet with sweat, despite the cold air that stung her face and pierced her lungs. She ran, as fast as she could. Each snapping twig made her heart jump. Every sound around her made her pause for a moment. A moment was all she could spare. Slowly she kept moving, through the woods, following the hidden road to freedom. As she made her way Lovina found her mind wandering back to all of her most cherished memories with the community and everything she was giving up. The celebrations and family dinners. Just as she lost herself completely in her thoughts a sharp noise snapped her back to reality.

She looked around desperately for somewhere to hide. She could distinguish faint footsteps coming her way. Who could be out here this late, in the cold? Lovina was convinced that she was caught. Someone had overheard her speaking of her plan to Jebidiah, or worse he had outed her himself. She threw her knapsack into a large bush to her left and jumped behind. As she crouched on the ground crazy accusations filled her head, but she kept her blue eyes focused on the clearing before her. Was it Jebidiah who let slip her secret plan, or did someone else overhear? When a shadowy figure finally caught her eye in the woods, she waited with baited breath to identify her stalker.

Branches crunched beneath his feet as the man emerged into the grassy clearing, uncloaked by the light of the moon. Lovina's jaw dropped and her heart raced at what felt like a thousand beats a second. She no longer needed to hide, she no longer had any fear or doubt about the path that she had chosen.

"Jebidiah!" she exclaimed, sprinting as fast as her legs could carry her toward him. A smile exploded across his face as she jumped carelessly into his outstretched arms. Jebidiah wrapped his muscular arms around her. He grasped her as tight as he could, never wanting to part again. She let her body melt into his. There they stood, nestled in each other's arms for several moments before severing their sensual embrace.

"I could not let you go, Lovina. I love you." Jebidiah confessed. She stared into his beaming blue eyes, looking down upon her. There was only one thing that she could respond.

"I love you too," she answered. Her eyes welled up with blissful tears that soon began running, one by one, down her soft cheeks. Jebidiah reached forward and wiped them away with his calloused hands. One of her arms drew back, reaching up to run her fingers through his mess of tangled hair, damp with sweat. Still stunned by his sudden appearance, she was nothing but ecstatic to see him.

At that moment, Jebidiah leaned down and kissed her soft, cherry lips for the first time, basking in the cool blanket of moonlight penetrating the canopy. Lovina could not believe her luck as she stood in the middle of the trees, in the arms of her love. She had been sure, not hours ago, that she had lost the love of her life forever. Now, she was on her way to making a new life for herself, in a new world, with the man of her dreams.

She leaned in closer to his warm silhouette, grasping at the fabric of his coat. She savored his touch, something she thought she had lost forever in the sands of time. His hand brushed her now flushing cheeks. He traced down her neck and over her petite shoulder. Her hand found its place against his pounding chest. And hers against his.

Jebidiah brushed a lock of hair from Lovina's ear.

"We must go now," he whispered softly to her. Stepping back from him, she nodded in agreement. She would no longer need to start her new life alone, they were together at last. He picked up her knapsack and hauled it onto his back.

"Come," he ushered Lovina back onto her path. Toward the city for the last time. As they neared the bustling hub, she witnessed the blanket of light illuminating the town. Never had she seen something so beautiful. Never had she felt so free.

ADA

Chapter 1

Ada looked at the letter she held in her hands. Her heart was beating hard. Part of herself was questioning the idea of even doing this. She was going to leave behind everything familiar, as terrible as it might be right now, for a man she had never met before. However, his letter and all his previous ones had looked kind enough.

"Ada,

It will be a pleasure to meet you. I have enjoyed conversing with you, and I will be waiting to meet you in the train station on the tenth of October. I hope you will have a safe journey.

Rainer"

While Rainer was usually a lot wordier, their letters had become shorter as they worked out the details of her travel.

"Dear God," Ada said, praying aloud as she finished packing her trunk. "I think you have really given me something special with Rainer. I pray that you would please help me have a safe journey and take away these fears that are plaguing me. Thank you for your mercy. Amen."

Ada sat on her bed as she stared at her trunk. It was not often that a women left a well settled Eastern town to go out West on the idea that they were going to marry a strange man, but Ada had always been one for adventure. Besides, leaving this town behind would let her leave her secret behind. There was no way it could follow her.

Ada took a deep breath. She would soon be able to leave everything behind. The trunk seemed to be full of everything she would need. She didn't even need to look around her room. It was completely empty. She had entered the house with only this trunk of things, and she had not had an opportunity to acquire any new belongings. Ada had already informed her landlady that she would be leaving. The woman had inquired about where she was going, but Ada had skirted around the answer. It was better that no one knew; her landlady tended to enjoy talking about the most interesting bits of news in regards to her tenants a bit too much for Ada's taste.

Ada smiled at the pile of letters she had from Rainer. They had been conversing over two months' time, and she felt as though she already knew him.

"Now, I just need to wait until my train leaves," Ada said, as the hours stretched before her. There would be no one to take leave of.

The next morning, Ada was happy to finally board the train. She had never been on a train before, and she was excited to see what it was like. She smiled to herself as she imagined what Rainer might look like. She had asked him to describe himself, but he only said that he had dark hair and dark eyes. Ada felt like her heart might recognize the man she had met through the letters. After all, if everything went well, they were to be married.

Ada's heart raced. Was she ready for marriage? She had to be. This was the only way to escape her hometown.

"Where are you going?" The woman sitting across from her asked amiably. Her voice startled Ada, and Ada put her hand over her heart.

"I'm sorry. I was completely distracted," Ada said. She smiled. "I'm going to Topeka, Kansas. And where are you going?"

"Denver, Colorado. My journey should be a fair bit longer than yours."

Ada smiled. "Are you visiting or moving?"

"Visiting," the woman nodded. "I grew up in Denver, but I wanted to move East when I got old enough to go out on my own."

Ada smiled. This woman had wanted to move East, and Ada had wanted to move West, each one escaping from where they had grown up. "I'm moving," Ada offered. "I grew up in. . . New York, but it was time for me to move on."

The woman smiled. "Well, I wish you good luck. Moving to a new part of the country can be a very difficult venture."

"Thank you," Ada said, her stomach rolling over. Perhaps it had been difficult for this woman, but anything would be better than her life in New York. She would finally be free to be herself and start over.

Ada passed the journey looking out the window and eating occasionally, but the hours stretched on. Ada felt as though she would never arrive in Topeka.

"What time should we arrive in Topeka?" she asked a man working on the train the next day.

"We are running a little behind schedule," the man said, glancing at his wristwatch. "I think we should arrive any time between four and five o'clock this evening."

Ada nodded. She hoped Rainer wouldn't mind waiting so long. She knew that she hated waiting, but at least when she was on the train, time seemed to pass more easily. However, her body was aching from spending the night sleeping in a sitting up position. Ada just wanted to arrive and sleep in a nice bed.

"I'm sorry," Ada said, stopping the same man as he made another round through the train. "What time is it?"

"1:30," the man replied.

Ada nodded. "Thank you." The time was passing more quickly than she had thought it would. Although lunchtime had already passed, Ada didn't feel the least tinges of hunger. She wondered how Rainer would act upon meeting her. Would he be affectionate right away or more cautious? Ada was naturally cautious, but she felt as though she already knew this stranger.

However, when it was time for Ada to deboard the train, what she saw was nothing like anything she had imagined.

Chapter 2

Ada scanned the crowd. She had never even seen a photo of this man. She assumed they did not have the kind of equipment out here in Topeka to even make a picture. However, there was one man in the crowd who just made her smile. He had dark hair, but Ada couldn't see his eyes. He was taller than a majority of the people.

Ada's heart fell as soon as she saw him talking to a woman. It couldn't be Rainer then. Ada took a deep breath and scanned the crowd again. She shouldn't be disappointed. Why was she disappointed? She had no right to feel disappointed just because Rainer wasn't the first handsome man she ran into.

There were two other men on one side who both had dark hair. One of them could easily be Rainer, but they weren't looking in her direction. Shouldn't they be looking for her? Was she supposed to approach random men and ask if they were named Rainer? This was ridiculous.

Ada let her eye wander back to that first man. He was looking right at her. He smiled and started striding over to her.

"Are you Ada?" he asked.

Ada's heart leaped, and the smile that popped onto her face was involuntarily. "Yes, I'm Ada. You must be Rainer then?"

The man nodded and awkwardly offered his hand. Ada felt strange shaking this man's hand like they had just made a business deal, but a hug would certainly not be appropriate at this time.

"It is such a pleasure to meet you," Rainer said. He looked down at her trunk. "Do you have any more things?"

"That's everything," Ada replied.

"Let's go then," Rainer said, turning and looking back. Ada saw that the woman she had first seen talking to Rainer was still standing there next to a pile of her things. Ada had assumed that Rainer was simply talking to her to find out if she was Ada. If that wasn't the case, why were there two women here for Rainer?

Ada wanted to ask, but she didn't feel comfortable enough yet. Instead, she asked a different question. "Where are we going?"

"I thought," Rainer said, turning back to look her full in the face. His face was chiseled and clean shaven. Ada liked the way he looked. "I thought I would take you to my mother's house. She has offered you a place to stay. I just finished constructing my own cabin, but I don't think it's quite a home yet. I thought letting you stay in my mother and father's house would be a good place for you as we get to know one another."

Ada had heard horror stories about men who had met their women in the stations and married them that same day. Ada was glad that Rainer wanted to take his time. "I think it sounds very thoughtful of you to have planned this out," Ada said. She smiled up at him. "I'm ready to go with you."

Rainer scooped up Ada's suitcase and led her back over to the other woman.

"Ada, this is Kaya. Kaya, this is Ada."

"Pleased to meet you," Kaya said.

"You as well," Ada said, dropping a curtsy. Kaya stared at her strangely, and Ada wondered if her customs were out of place in this Western town. Ada desperately searched for a reason that this woman was going with them. Perhaps she was a family member. Rainer grabbed one of Kaya's bags, and she carried the smaller bag with her.

"I'll drop you off first, Kaya," Rainer said as he placed the suitcases in the back of his carriage. "Let me help you ladies up." Kaya bustled in to be let up first. Ada demurely followed behind. Rainer hoisted her up just as he had done for Kaya. He then went to the opposite side of the carriage and took the horses' reins. Kaya was in the middle.

Ada started becoming angry. She was supposed to be coming out to Topeka to meet a ranch owner who was free to marry. What then was this other woman doing here at the same time? Surely, Rainer had not been writing to more than one woman? Ada couldn't bear the thought. Returning to New York simply was not an option.

"How far do you live from the station?" Ada asked. She leaned forward a little so she could see Rainer around Kaya.

"It's not far. About half an hour's journey." Rainer immediately turned to Kaya. "The hotel is about ten minutes from here. I promise you that the owners are very friendly. I know them personally, and you will feel quite comfortable there."

Kaya smiled at Rainer, and Ada seethed. She was normally a very laid back person, but this woman was coming in and stomping all over her fairy tale. What was she supposed to do? Push Kaya out of the carriage and slide over next to Rainer? Ada shook her head and took a deep breath. She silently prayed and asked God for patience. She asked him for some of his mercy on this girl.

Ada felt a lot better after giving God her worries. The ride was short, and a few minutes later as the carriage rested on the edge of town, Rainer jumped out. He helped Kaya down then gathered her bags.

"I'll be right back. I'm just going to take these bags inside for Kaya. Will you be alright waiting here?"

Ada nodded, feeling the jealousy cropping up. Rainer started walking toward the hotel. Kaya stayed behind for a few minutes.

"Are you courting Rainer?" she asked in a low voice.

Ada paused. Were they courting? It was more like something more. They already knew they were going to get married. "Not exactly," Ada said, trying to explain. "I came to Topeka. I just met him, but. . ."

Kaya nodded. "Okay, I should probably go." She pointed at the hotel across the street. "Rainer is probably waiting."

But we're going to get married! Ada wanted to shout at Kaya, but Kaya was already bustling inside. Ada folded her arms and waited as the sun sank below the horizon. The sunset was beautiful, but Ada didn't enjoy it. She tried to reason with herself, but her idea of a happy ending seemed to be fast fading. She didn't want Kaya getting in her way, and she didn't know how long Kaya was planning to be here. Kaya's open question made her intentions clear enough.

Chapter 3

When Rainer got back in the carriage, all of the things that Ada wanted to say to him, warning him about Kaya's possible intentions were fading out of her mind. After all, even though she had come out here to marry Rainer, they might not fall in love. He might discover that their personalities were simply too different. After all, he didn't seem very picky or jealous like she was.

"Sorry about the delay," Rainer smiled at her. "I felt bad for her. She said that she didn't know how to find the hotel."

"Of course," Ada said. "It was kind of you to help someone you don't know at all." She emphasized those words to demonstrate the difference between herself and this new woman. "The sunset was beautiful."

Rainer smiled at her. "Isn't it? I love the way God puts a touch of beauty in everything he makes."

Ada smiled genuinely, feeling the stress seep away. "I agree. I'm glad that the countryside is so beautiful. While it is a far cry from what I know in New York, I somehow feel at home here."

"Perhaps it is because God created us to be at home no matter where we are in his world."

Ada liked the way that Rainer mentioned God and talked about him as though he was his best friend. "I know you have a lot of cows and few bulls from your letters," Ada said. "But I want to learn more about your farm." Ada sent him a sideways glance. She didn't have to feign interest. She already felt it strongly. "Tell about what you do every day. You're not confined to a small piece of paper or a telegram."

Rainer smiled. "Well, I love my cows, you know. I might get to jabbering away about them for hours at a time. Just tell me when you get bored."

Ada smiled and agreed. Rainer then began telling her about what he did on his farm, how he milked the cows, fixed the fences, and did anything else required of him. Ada was very interested in how he milked the cows.

"I actually have a boy who comes over and helps me with the milking," Rainer explained. "If you're interested in helping, I definitely need the hands."

"I'm not an expert milker," Ada laughed, "but I would be very interested in trying it out."

"Maybe after a few lessons, you'll find you are a natural."

Ada was disappointed to see them pulling into the drive in front of a log house. "This is my family's house," Rainer explained.

"Where do you live?" Ada asked.

Rainer put his arm around her and pointed to the West. "If you look, you might be able to distinguish my house against the moon's light."

Ada was more focused on how his arm felt around her shoulders. She tried to find the house, moving her face around. "I think I see it," Ada said, even though she wasn't sure.

"It's about another fifteen minutes from here by road, unless you get to galloping on a horse."

"Now horse riding is something I can do," Ada said. She was thankful for the horse riding lessons she had had when she was young.

"Let's go inside," Rainer said. He brought her into the house and introduced his mother and father. They were just laying out dinner, and Ada's stomach rumbled. That lunch she had not eaten meant she was empty and ready to eat.

Ada tried to be polite to everyone. "Let me get Ada's trunk," Rainer said. "I'll be back." He went outside and briefly left Ada by herself. She smiled at everyone nervously.

"It's nice to have you here," Rainer's mother- Rachel- said.

Ada nodded. "Thank you for being so accommodating. I know it must put you out to have a stranger among you."

Rainer's father, Benjamin, shook his head. "No, I much prefer it this way. It's better you stay here while you and Rainer get to know one another, before you get married and find out that your letters were poor representations of who you really are."

Ada was silent. She could tell that Rainer's father did not approve of their method of finding each other. She merely looked around and noted that the house was mostly quiet. There were no small children. Ada was under the impression that Western families always had a lot of children.

"Do you have any more children?" Ada asked politely.

Rachel nodded. "Yes, we have five children total. Three have married and moved out. Rainer just finished building his own house, and Ella is probably out there with our baby pigs. She is crazy about baby animals."

"How old is Ella?" Ada asked.

"Sixteen," Rachel replied. Ada nodded and looked around the house as she stood awkwardly in the doorway. "Come," Rachel said. "Sit down, and I will serve you a plate."

"Thank you," Ada said. "But perhaps I should wait for Rainer first."

She saw Rachel give Benjamin a look, but she could only guess what was passing between both of Rainer's parents. When Rainer finally came in with his sister in tow, they all sat down and ate dinner. Ada found Ella very friendly, even though she was five years younger than herself. Ada knew that she would get along well with Ella. Now, Ada only had to worry about how things would work out without Rainer.

"I am going to ride over to my house," Rainer said. He made eye contact with Ada. "Would you like to go outside with me for a few minutes?"

Ada nodded and tried to keep the smile off her face. She had been wanting a few minutes to speak privately with Rainer. They sat outside the cabin on two stools. The only light came from the fire inside that leaked light through the cracks.

"Would you really like to help with milking tomorrow?" Rainer asked.

"I would," Ada hesitated. "But my journey has tired me out. I think I may need to sleep late tomorrow. But perhaps the next day. . ."

Rainer nodded. "Of course. Don't worry. Another day will work just fine. How about after I finish everything that needs to be taken care of on the farm, I could drive you into town? If you are missing anything or you find that you need something, we can get it."

"I really don't need anything," Ada protested.

Rainer held up his hand. "Then I shall get you something you don't need. There is a woman in town who makes delicious ice cream. I'd like to get you a cone."

Ada smiled. She liked the idea. "Okay, I'll be ready then."

"Good night," Rainer said. He stood as did Ada. There was a moment of awkwardness as they tried to decide how to say goodbye. They finally both waved. Rainer mounted his horse and disappeared into the darkness. Ada sat outside for a few minutes by herself, thinking over her day. When she started nodding off, she realized she should go to bed before she fell off the stool and hurt herself.

Chapter 4

The next day, Ada waited anxiously for the time when Rainer would arrive. He did not disappoint, and he came over just in time for the midday meal. After they had eaten, he told her he would ready the carriage and take her for ice cream.

"Oh, can't I go?" Ella asked.

Rainer didn't even take a moment to think about his answer. "Of course. I can't keep my baby sister ice cream free."

"I'm not your baby sister."

"Oh, do I have another sister younger than you?" Rainer teased, pretending to look around. His voice dropped as though they were discussing an important, secret matter. "Is Ma going to have another child?"

Ella laughed. "I wish she would, but you know that won't happen. Let me go change into my nice shoes."

"You don't mind, do you?" Rainer asked, turning to Ada.

Ada shook her head, even though she did mind. She had wanted to experience this first outing alone with Rainer. She felt as though if she went out with brother and sister, she would immediately feel let out of all their jokes.

"Let's go," Rainer said. Ella hurried toward the carriage, but Rainer purposely boosted Ada first before helping his sister in. Ada felt her cheeks warm as Rainer pushed into the carriage and sat right next to her. She could feel his leg pressed against hers, and Ada swallowed a few times to keep her mouth from growing dry.

Rainer teased Ella about her money for ice cream, asking her how she planned to buy one when she didn't have any money. Ada smiled. These two were close, and that said something about Rainer. Ada knew there were seven years between the two, but she liked how close they were. She liked the jokester, generous side of him that she hadn't quite been able to grasp through his letters.

When they reached town, Rainer helped them both down. He walked in the middle and held his arm out. Ada looped her arm through Rainer's and smiled as they chatted. The more she talked to him, the more she felt as though this was the kind of man she could spend the rest of her life with.

They reached the ice cream parlor and stepped inside. The parlor only offered five different flavors and was very different from the pharmacy where Ada got her ice cream in New York. She looked at the flavors and knew immediately that she wanted chocolate. Nothing else appealed to her. Even though there were not a menagerie of flavors, Ella took perhaps ten minutes scanning the flavors.

"What are you getting, Ada?" she finally asked.

"Chocolate," Ada answered easily. "I love anything chocolate, and I probably indulged in it too much in my earlier days." Ada stopped herself before she went too deep into her memories.

"I think chocolate is a good idea," Ella said. "I'll have chocolate as well," Ella said. Rainer ordered their ice creams and handed each of the cones to them paired with a gallant bow.

They sat down at a small table and began eating their ice cream. Rainer and Ella began talking about some of the latest town news. Ada listened in.

"I'm sorry," Rainer said, in the middle of saying something to his sister. "We must have been boring you incredibly. I didn't mean to make conversation about something you wouldn't know, but. . ."

"Please," Ada said, smiling. "Don't worry yourself about it. I am finding it quite interesting learning about my new town."

"So," Ella broke in. "Are you two really going to marry just because you wrote letters to each other?"

Ada's cheeks turned red. This was one of those questions that made the person speechless when they received it, but later on, they knew exactly how they would answer. Ada slid a look at Rainer who was smiling at her. "I guess that's what we're going to find out, Ella. Maybe you should keep your nose in your own business."

Ella gave her brother an annoyed look. "I just wanted to know. It seems a little strange to me."

"You seem a little strange to me," Rainer replied, ducking from his sister's retaliation. Ada stood and threw her napkin in the bin.

Rainer copied suit and held out his arm for her to use once again. Ada slipped her hand into the crook of his elbow as Ella caught up with them. "Did you discover you needed anything?" Rainer asked.

"Um, no, I have everything," Ada said, feeling strange about Rainer's freedom to spend money on anything she might request.

"Surely you need something. Perhaps you and Ella can go together into the general store. I do need to buy some meat. My icebox is almost empty. I shall leave you two here and meet you back in half an hour. Surely you can find something to occupy your time during then," Rainer said.

The two women nodded and watched Rainer took off with a purposeful stride. "Where would you like to go?" Ella asked.

Ada shrugged. "You know this town much better than I do. I might simply like to walk for a bit." The two girls got to know each other as they took a walk through the town. Ada enjoyed meeting new people. Many seemed to know Ella, and they all asked who her new friend was.

Ada found herself the center of attention. "Has the time passed yet?" she asked Ella. Ella nodded.

"I believe it has. Let's go back. If we are late, my brother won't be happy."

The two made their way back to the corner, and Ada was not happy when she saw who was standing there waiting for them. Rainer was talking with Kaya. Ada set her jaw, wanting to hang back so that Rainer wouldn't notice them. Maybe if they hung back, then she could see how Rainer acted when he didn't anyone was watching him.

Kaya laid her hand on Rainer's arm as she laughed. Rainer was laughing too, and Ada's stomach felt sick. What did he find so funny about this woman? What were they talking about?

Ella burst forward to join the two. "Has it been half an hour already? I feel like the time just flies. Ava and I didn't think you would be here yet."

Rainer nodded. "Yes, but don't worry. I haven't minded the waiting."

Ava hung back. She was really hurt by the fact that the one time that she left Rainer alone, he would start talking with this woman and let her put her hands all over him. She had a right to act hurt, but if she acted hurt, then there was no way she would be able to get Rainer's attention again.

Ava stepped forward. "It's nice to see you again, Kaya," Ava said, resisting offering a curtsy.

Ella looked confused. "You know this woman. I've never seen her before. Are you new in town?" Ella asked Kaya.

Kaya nodded. "Yes, I just came in yesterday on the train." She answered as one would answer an annoying pet that kept barking at her.

"Oh, are you going to be staying in town for long?" Ada was glad that Ella had the courage to ask all the questions on Ada's mind.

"Yes," Kaya nodded. "I just moved here. My family lived her when I was little. I thought it would be a good place to find a husband."

Ava couldn't believe Kaya was so open about her intentions, and even more than that, Ava couldn't believe that Rainer was not disgusted by Kaya's obvious desperation.

"So, you'll be here for a while then?" Rainer asked.

"If all goes well, then I hope to live here for the rest of my life," Kaya said, smiling in a sickly sweet way at Rainer.

Ava made a face then quickly changed her expression to a neutral one. She couldn't have Rainer asking her about why she was so resistant to this woman. Some men simply didn't understand. But then, Ava couldn't believe her ears.

"I'm sure my Ma wouldn't mind if I invited you for dinner sometime. I'll warn her, but I am fairly sure that any evening would be fine. She would hate for a new woman in town to be eating by herself every night."

Kaya smiled. "Of course," she smiled. "Thank you for your invitation. I shall be sure to accept your invitation one evening this week. It's not easy moving back to a town from your childhood. It seems as though most people don't remember me. They know of my parents, but that doesn't make it any easier for me."

Ava watched as Kaya successfully secured it. "I'm sure that is hard," Rainer agreed. "I can't imagine living somewhere far away from my family."

"Well," Rainer said, glancing at his watch. "The meat is going to get warm. We should probably go. I shall talk to you later." Ella and Ava said goodbye as well. As Ava was helped into the carriage this time, she didn't feel as happy as she had when they set out that morning.

Chapter 5

Ava spent the next three days exploring Rainer's farm. "I wasn't sure what I thought about a cattle farm," Ada said.

"Why?" Rainer said, giving her an odd look as though it was strange anyone could have a problem with cows.

"Because," Ada said. She smiled, because she knew how Rainer would react. "I've never seen a cow before."

"What?" Rainer's surprise soon gave way to laughter. "Don't they herd cattle where you live? There have to be fields close to the city."

Ada shook her head. "No. My landlady would buy fresh milk every morning, but the man who sold it didn't bring the cow along with him."

Rainer laughed. "I wouldn't bring my cows along either. I use them mostly for breeding, but when they don't have a baby, why wouldn't I take the milk?"

"Do you sell it?" Ada asked. "I haven't seen you coming down the streets making sales."

"I take it to the general store every morning. Mr. Baines buys it from me and sells it to his customers. I keep some of it to make butter. Do you know how to churn butter?"

Ada shook her head. "No, show me how."

Rainer laughed again. "I don't know how. I know the basic process. It includes a lot of movement, but I don't know the specific techniques. My ma can help you out in that area."

Rainer put his hand on his stomach. "I think my stomach is telling me it is supper time. Are you hungry?"

Ada nodded. She wanted to eat a private dinner with Rainer, but he always ate dinner at his ma's house. Ada wasn't quite sure why he had moved over there if he was going to spend some much time there.

They paused in the doorway of his house, and Ada looked around. As soon as she had first seen the house, she began imagining how she could put some touches of home in it. Ada turned back. Rainer was right behind her, and Ada smiled gently.

"When we live here," she ventured to say. "I will make you a special dinner every night."

"You will, will you?" Rainer asked, his thumb coming up and gently stroking her jaw. The touch made Ada feel nervous. She knew that she felt strongly for Rainer, but she had been unsure of his feelings until that very moment. "I think I'll enjoy that very much, a special dinner for the two of us."

"What do you like to eat?" Ada said, taking Rainer's rough hand between her own. She didn't want to go yet. She didn't want to walk across those fields and enter his mom's house, missing this romantic moment.

"My favorite? Oh, I love some good mashed potatoes with some homemade butter. That's my favorite." He looked down at her, and Ada suddenly realized how close they were standing. "But anything you cook, I would be happy to try."

Ada felt her breath come quickly. She looked down at Rainer's lips and back into his eyes. A smile twitched on his lips. He gently bent down and kissed her lips. Ada leaned into his lips and felt them softly part. When Rainer pulled back, his face was completely serious. But the moment Ada smiled, Rainer's face popped into a smile too.

Ada wanted to say something. She wanted to tell Rainer that his kiss had been everything she wanted it to be. She wanted to ask him when they were going to get married. She had come out here to be his bride, but Rainer seemed content to wait.

"Come on," Rainer said. "My ma will begin to wonder where we are."

Ada nodded and took Rainer's extended hand. They walked hand in hand the distance to his ma's house. It took them twenty minutes, and it took every ounce of Ada's strength not to jabber his ear off. She wanted to keep the silence and replay the moment in her head. Just a few minutes before they entered Rachel and Benjamin's cabin, Ada smiled at Rainer. He smiled at her, and Ada knew they shared a special secret.

When Ada stepped inside and saw Kaya seated comfortably at the table, Ada felt her stomach drop. Rainer let go of Ada's hand and went over to greet Kaya. Ada was cordial, but she could not bring herself to be friendly. Even though she was scolding her own behavior, Ada could not help but be jealous. Rainer seemed to be so friendly with Kaya, and he barely knew her.

"I am so glad you were able to find your way here," Rainer said. Kaya smiled back. She spotted Ada in the doorway and seemed confused, but she continued right on with her conversation with Rainer, not caring how Ada felt. Wasn't Ada going to marry Rainer? Hadn't he said as much? Why would he act so different now?

Ada swallowed as she realized that he hadn't mentioned it since in their letters. Maybe the only reason he hadn't married her yet was that he was distracted by Kaya. Maybe *that* was the whole reason it was taking them so long to "get to know each other."

Ada settled on the corner of the couch, wanting to know everything that passed between Kaya and Rainer, yet not wanting to hear how amiable Rainer sounded the whole time. Ada started worrying about what would happen should Rainer decide not to marry her. Ada felt as if she was choking in the heat of the fire. Ada stood and walked over to the doorway where the cool air was coming in. She couldn't go back to New York. She had already been shunned by her family, what was left of it.

Ada swallowed over and over, licking her lips and trying to make herself feel normal. Would she have to stay in Topeka and watch Rainer and Kaya have children together? Ada stepped outside to brush away the two tears that rushed out without permission.

"God," Ada said quietly. "Please, please." She didn't know what else to say as she begged God for mercy on her situation. "I can't go back, but I wouldn't have the money to stay here. I used up almost everything staying with the landlord in New York. Please have mercy. I thought this was what you wanted for me."

Ada was silent and felt a gentle breeze that seemed to come straight from heaven to her. It helped her feel peaceful. It was as though that wind carried the words "Trust Me."

"I'm trying," Ada protested, then she realized she wasn't really trying at all. She had just assumed that everything was going wrong, so she began to let her fears take over. "God, help me trust you," Ada said. She took a deep breath and was just about to step inside when she saw Rainer standing in the doorway.

"Is everything alright, Ada?" he asked.

Ada nodded, trying to force a smile for him. Rainer's smile was not forced by any means. "Come on," he said. "My ma has dinner ready, and she doesn't want it to get cold. You're hungry, aren't you?"

Ada nodded as Rainer took her hand and led her in to a spot on the bench beside himself. Ella and Kaya sat across from them. They all held hands to bless the meal, then Ada began eating. Rainer amiably made conversation with them all. Every time he turned and looked at Ada, she felt warmth in her stomach.

Chapter 6

Ada was disappointed when Rainer offered to drive Kaya back into town. She said that she had asked someone to drive her out there, but she did not have a way back. It was the perfect excuse, of course, but Ada was still disappointed. She did not like the idea of Rainer being with Kaya alone.

Ada dejectedly changed into her nightdress and combed out her hair. She was sharing a bed with Ella, and Ella was getting ready for bed as well.

"If I didn't know that my brother had sent for you to marry him, I would think he was quite taken with that Kaya."

Ella's words were not the ones Ada wanted to hear. Ada nodded, not being able to add her thoughts without crying.

Ella turned and saw Ada's serious face. "Don't worry. My brother's just always friendly to everyone." She seemed to be saying the exact opposite of what she had said only a moment earlier.

"I prefer not to talk about it," Ada said. "I'm very tired, and I need to get up for milking tomorrow." With that, Ada lay down on the bed and shut her eyes, pretending to be asleep.

The next morning, Ada showed up early for the milking. She tied an apron around her waist and made her way out to the barn. By now, she was comfortable around the cows. While she still was scared that one of them would step on her, she didn't shy away from the smell anymore.

"Good morning!" Rainer said, stepping out of the barn.

"Oh, am I late?" Ada asked, her eyes dropping to the ground.

Rainer shook his head. "You're right on time." He came forward and took one of her hands. "Come on, let's get this milking done, so I can let them out to pasture."

Ada sat down on the stool that was set up in her milking stall. Across the aisle, Rainer was milking another cow. His more experienced hands finished three cows in the time it took her to do one, but Ada was learning. She worked out her stress as she finished milking the cow. She needed to talk with Rainer about Kaya. She had to know how Rainer felt. If he felt something for Kaya, she would need another plan, because she couldn't stay in that town either. With about five cows left, Rainer suggested she go inside and make breakfast while he finished up and let them all out to pasture.

Ada quickly whipped up some eggs. She got out the bread she had made the day before and spread some jam on it. She placed the food on the table and waited for Rainer to come in.

"Let's pray," Rainer said. He bowed his head and thanked God for the food then began digging in.

"Rainer," Ada said softly. He looked up. "You know, I've been here more than a week, and we still haven't talked of getting married. I came out here to be your bride, didn't I?"

Rainer smiled at her. "Getting impatient, are you?"

"No," Ada immediately protested. "I just, I'm confused, what with your behavior toward Kaya, and no mention of a marriage."

"Surely you didn't think I wasn't going to marry you," Rainer protested. Ada shrugged. She felt silly admitting it now. Rainer stood and left his breakfast at the table as he pulled her to her feet. He forced her to look into his eyes. "I don't want you to be confused anymore," Rainer said. "Yes, I am going to marry you. I would never bring you away from your hometown, your family, everything, unless my intentions were true."

Ada swallowed, her secret weighing heavily on her. Could Rainer really love her if he didn't know the truth about everything that she had done before she came to Topeka? A part of her whispered that the past was in the past; all had been forgiven. But another part of her was nervous. She was worried Rainer would eventually find out and never trust her again.

Ada pulled Rainer into a hug and laid her head on his chest. She could feel his heart beating. Rainer wrapped his arms around her and gently kissed the top of her head.

"Ada," Rainer said gently. "I will marry you today if that is what you want."

Ada's heart almost felt like it was going to stop beating right then. She couldn't. He had to know, No, he didn't. Ada went back and forth in her mind, and Rainer pulled back from her, easing her chin up as he watched the emotions pass over her face.

"Something's wrong," he said, shaking his head.

This was all wrong! Why hadn't she just agreed as soon as he said it?

"Do you find yourself unhappy here?" Rainer asked, lifting his eyebrows.

Ada shook her head hurriedly. "No, I love your family, and I lo-" Ada broke off. "I enjoy getting to know you. I couldn't imagine my future in any other city with any other family."

"Then, what's the trouble?" Rainer asked.

Ada took a deep breath. She felt the unasked for tears rising to the surface. She was ruining everything! Rainer took another step backward as though her tears were scaring him. He shook his head. Ada wanted to reach out and grab him, force him to hug her again as he had been doing, force him to love her and ignore her secrets.

"I'm sorry," Ada said, quickly wiping her fingers under her eyes. "We should eat up the breakfast before it gets cold."

Rainer sat down at the table and began eating, but Ada found that she could not eat. She stirred the food around on her plate then asked Rainer if he would like some more. He shook his head. "Look," he said. "I know it must be hard being away from your family. If this isn't right for you, you should decide that now before we get married."

Ada's stomach clenched up. She couldn't imagine feeling as strongly about a man as she felt about Rainer, but he seemed to be distancing himself from her. Ada knew that if she wanted to hold onto this man, she would have to tell him everything.

Chapter 7

"Rainer," Ada said, following him to the door. "I need to talk to you."

Rainer turned around and studied her. "What's wrong?" he asked.

Ada wanted to take his hand and pull him back to the kitchen table. She didn't want to have this conversation while he was standing in the doorway, glancing out to the barn, and thinking about his chores. At the same time, she didn't have the courage to be bold and bring him back to the table.

"I am responsible for my sister's death," Ada said.

Rainer raised his eyebrows then did exactly what Ada had been wanting. He guided her back to the kitchen table, and they sat facing each other. "What happened?" Rainer asked.

Ada tried to swallow back the tears, but they seemed insistent on coming anyway. The tears spilled over, and Ada sobbed as she told her story. "It happened about three months ago. The weather was warm, and my mom asked me to watch my younger sister. Penelope was her name." Ada swallowed slowly as Rainer put his hand on top of hers.

"I decided to take her swimming. We stopped by my friend's house. I asked her if she wanted to come. She came with us. Penelope was three years old. When we got to the pond, there were plenty of children who had the same idea. I shooed Penelope into the water, preferring to talk with my friend instead of watching her. I heard children's shouts and saw Penelope in the middle of the pond. She went under the water. I know now, it must have been the tenth or twelfth time she went under. She was drowning. I stood watching her. I wasn't able to move. I counted the seconds, waiting for her to come up. She never did. I finally swam out and found her. . .her body. She was dead."

Ada was crying, and she lost her ability to talk. She laid her face on her hands and sobbed. How could she have been so thoughtless? If she had just looked at her sister instead of her friend, if she had been more careful, or moved more quickly, she could have saved her. Rainer wrapped his arms around her, but it didn't make Ada feel any better.

When her sobs had finished wracking through her body, Ada looked up and wiped her face. "My parents told me I was not welcome in their house any longer. I had to move out. I wanted to come here to escape. I enjoyed talking with you through our letters, but," Ada swallowed, wanting to tell the truth completely. "Honestly, I did not care who the man was, as long as I could get away from my hometown and start over. I didn't like the people looking at me and whispering. I wanted to be normal, accepted, and loved."

Rainer gently rubbed the top of her hand. He didn't look angry or condemning. He looked like he might understand her. "Ada," he said, causing her to look into his eyes, urgently hoping he would be able to forgive her.

"I would never hold such a mistake against you," he said. "What happened was an accident, not something you purposely did."

Ada furrowed her brows.

"I'm sure you loved Penelope, am I right?"

"I never showed her how much I loved her," Ada said, her voice full of regret. She suddenly gave a sob that had a smile. "I remember how she would get home from going out with either me or my mother, and she would throw her shoes into the air and begin running around the house. She hated shoes."

Rainer smiled. "They can be quite cumbersome for a little child."

"I just," Ada was back to thinking on her current situation. "I want to start over. I didn't want you to know. I felt like you might decide I wasn't ready. But, since I came here, I realized that I don't only like the idea of leaving my town, I really like you."

Rainer kissed her forehead. "You know what, Ada? I like you as well. In fact, I really want to marry you."

"Marry me," Ada repeated the words like a child fascinated with the idea. "Yes, please," Ada said.

Rainer stood and took both of her hands. He pulled her closer and kissed her lips with such promise that Ada was left breathless.

"Yes," Rainer said. "I'll marry you. You can be my wife, and I will be your husband. We can have a family together."

Ada smiled widely. "Yes," she said. She hugged Rainer tightly. She wanted to shout. She felt so filled with joy. "We will get married and have a life together."

"Forever and ever," Rainer whispered gently. "Ada, would you have time in your busy day today to go to the courthouse?"

Ada's stomach dropped as she nodded. This was really happening. She was going to marry this man. "I think I can perhaps make time for you," she teased, her fears relived from having told him her darkest secret.

"Do you have something special to wear?" Rainer asked.

Ada nodded. "Yes, I have a special white dress that I sewed myself."

Rainer smiled. "Tell my Ma and Pa to drive you into town. I will meet you at the courthouse at ten o'clock."

Ada wrapped her arms around Rainer and smiled again, delirious with joy. "I shall tell them right now." She took a few running steps toward his parents' cabin before she turned back. "I forgot something." Rainer looked confused for a moment, but then Ada kissed him, her soft lips pressed against his. She pulled back, and he was smiling widely at her.

"I'm going to marry you," Ada said.

Rainer nodded. "Yes, you are. Now, go. Go get ready!"